Police Officers

Izzi Howell

W

Franklin Watts
First published in Great Britain in paperback in 2022 by The Watts Publishing Group
Copyright © The Watts Publishing Group, 2018

Produced for Franklin Watts by
White-Thomson Publishing Ltd
www.wtpub.co.uk

ISBN: 978 1 4451 6492 2
10 9 8 7 6 5 4 3 2 1

Credits
Series Editor: Izzi Howell
Series Designer: Rocket Design (East Anglia) Ltd
Designer: Clare Nicholas
Literacy Consultant: Kate Ruttle

The publisher would like to thank the following for permission to reprowduce their pictures: Alamy: Dorset Media Service 4, Mark Harvey 17; Getty: zodebala cover, kaarsten 5 and 21t, Andrew_Howe 6, John Patrick Fletcher/Action Plus 8, Blend Images - Hill Street Studios/Matthew Palmer 12, Richard Hutchings 13, zoka74 14, joebelanger 15, Bombaert 18, ymgerman 19t, Thinkstock 19b, Ian_Redding 21b, Photodisc 22; Shutterstock: Leonard Zhukovsky title page and 7t, Gabriel Petrescu 7b, Sean Locke Photography 9, photka 10, marcyano 11, Dmitry Kalinovsky 16, KellyNelson 20.

Every attempt has been made to clear copyright. Should there be any inadvertent omission please apply to the publisher for rectification.

Printed in Dubai

Franklin Watts
An imprint of
Hachette Children's Group
Part of The Watts Publishing Group
Carmelite House
50 Victoria Embankment
London EC4Y 0DZ

An Hachette UK Company
www.hachette.co.uk
www.franklinwatts.co.uk

All words in **bold** appear in the glossary on page 23.

Contents

Who are police officers?

Police officers keep people safe. They try to stop **crimes** from happening. They also **solve** crimes.

You might see police officers in your town or city.
▼

Police officers help at car accidents. They direct traffic around the accident so that the road is not blocked for long.

▲ Police officers also direct cars to stop traffic jams.

Uniform

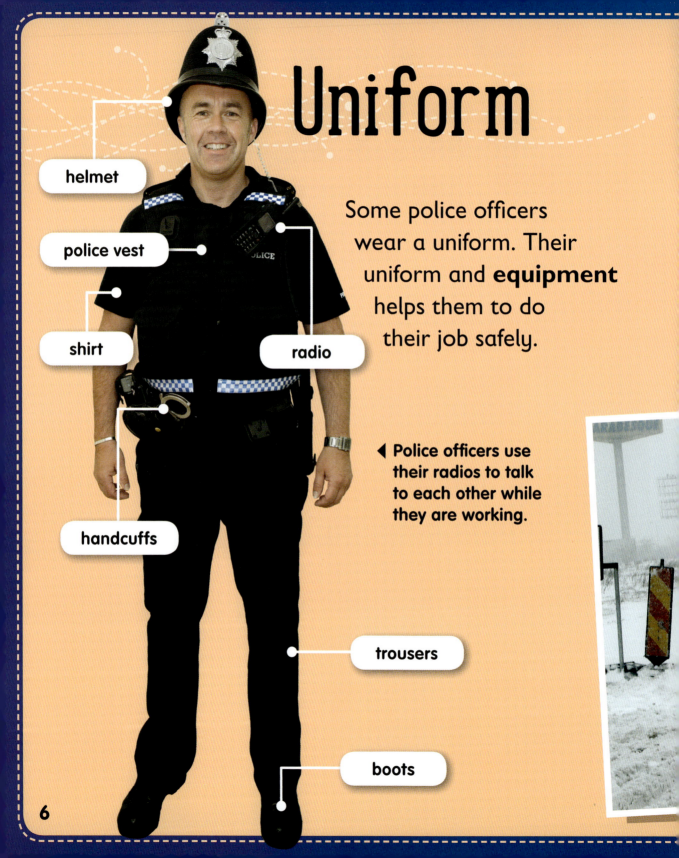

helmet

police vest

shirt

radio

handcuffs

Some police officers wear a uniform. Their uniform and **equipment** helps them to do their job safely.

◀ Police officers use their radios to talk to each other while they are working.

trousers

boots

The police uniform can change with the weather.

These police officers are wearing shirts with short sleeves, hats and sunglasses in the hot summer. ▶

◀ This police officer is wearing a warm hat, coat and gloves in the snow.

Why do you think police officers wear yellow jackets?

On patrol

Police officers walk around our towns and cities **on patrol**. They look for people who need help.

▼ These police officers are on patrol.

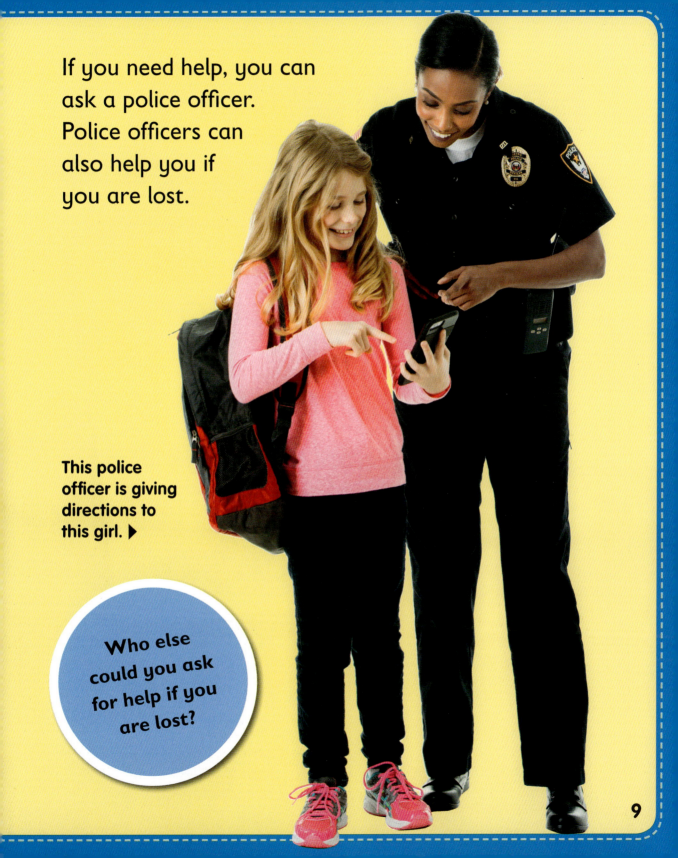

If you need help, you can ask a police officer. Police officers can also help you if you are lost.

This police officer is giving directions to this girl. ▶

Who else could you ask for help if you are lost?

Emergency!

People sometimes need the police in an **emergency**. In the UK, they ring 999 on the phone and ask for the police. In Australia, the phone number for the police is 000.

You can also ring 999 if someone is badly hurt or if there is a fire. ▶

Police officers come to help as soon as they can. They have a flashing light and a **siren** on their cars. This lets other drivers know that the police car needs to go in front of them.

Police cars drive quickly to an emergency. ▼

What does a police siren sound like?

The crime scene

Police officers visit places where crimes have happened. This place is called the **crime scene**.

Police officers take notes about the crime scene. ▼

Police officers put up tape to stop people touching the crime scene. ▶

12

▲ Police officers can learn more about crimes by asking people questions.

Police officers need to find out information about the crime. They talk to people who saw the crime.

What kind of questions do you think police officers ask?

Evidence

Criminals leave behind **evidence** at a crime scene, such as their fingerprints or hair. Scientists are **trained** to look for this evidence.

This scientist has found a fingerprint at a crime scene. ▼

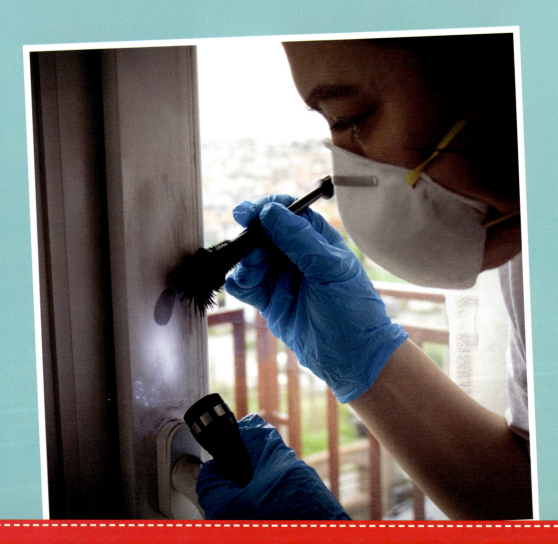

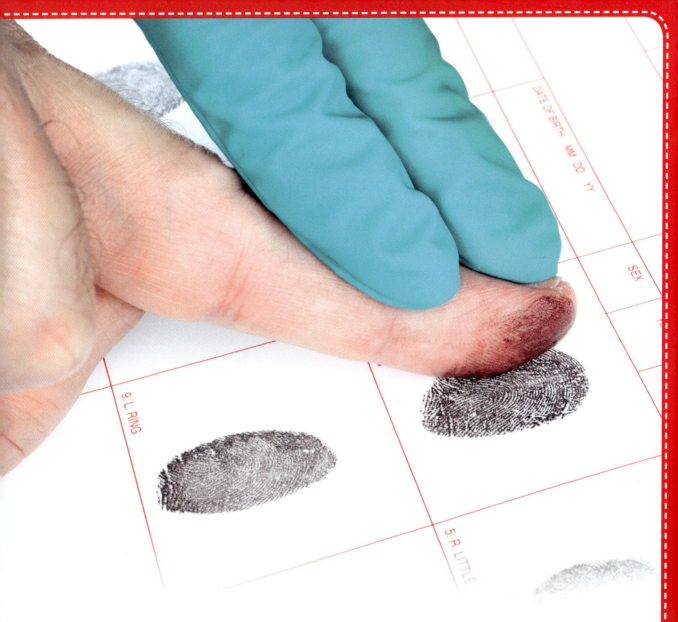

Evidence helps police officers understand what happened during a crime. It helps them work out who might be a **suspect**.

▲

Suspects have to show the police their fingerprints. The police check if they are the same as the fingerprints from the crime scene.

Police station

Police officers work from the police station. They look at evidence and try to solve crimes.

This police officer is looking at video from a street camera to learn more about a crime.

▼

Police officers talk to suspects at the police station. Some suspects aren't allowed to leave the police station. They stay at the police station in **cells**.

This man is answering the police officers' questions. ▼

Vehicles

Police officers use different **vehicles** to move around. In towns and cities, they usually drive cars. Some police officers ride bikes or motorbikes.

▼ Motorbikes allow police officers to move more quickly through busy streets.

In some places, police officers have to travel in different vehicles.

Police officers patrol rivers in boats. ▶

◀ Police officers use helicopters to follow criminals.

Animals

Police dogs have been trained to help police officers. They use their sense of smell to find missing people or criminals.

The police dog leads the police officer towards the smell of a person.

▼

Have you ever seen a police dog? Where was it?

Some police officers ride horses
on patrol. They can move fast.
Being high up helps them to see better.

These police officers
are patrolling the
busy centre of New
York City in the USA
on horseback. ▶

◀ Police officers ride
horses to patrol
big open areas,
such as parks.

Quiz

Test how much you remember.

Check your answers on page 24.

1 Name three things that police officers wear as their uniform.

2 What phone number should you ring to talk to the police in an emergency?

3 How do police cars show that they are going to an emergency?

4 Why is evidence important for police officers?

5 Which moves through traffic more quickly – a police car or a police motorbike?

6 What do police dogs do?

Glossary

cell – a small room in a police station where a suspect stays

crime – something bad that is not allowed by law, such as stealing something

crime scene – the place where a crime happened

emergency – an important or dangerous situation that people need to sort out quickly

equipment – things that are used for an activity or job

evidence – an object that gives you more information about a crime

on patrol – looking for danger or problems in an area

siren – something that makes a loud sound

solve – to find the answer to something

suspect – someone who may have committed a crime

train – to teach someone how to do something

vehicle – a type of transport, such as a car or a bus

Index

Answers:

1: Helmet, shirt, trousers, badge, handcuffs, radio, vest, boots; 2: 999/000; 3: They have a flashing light and a siren; 4: It helps them understand what happened during a crime and who might be a suspect; 5: A police motorbike; 6: Use their sense of smell to find missing people or criminals

Teaching notes:

Children who are reading Book band Gold or above should be able to enjoy this book with some independence. Other children will need more support.

Before you share the book:

- Introduce the idea of emergency services - people you call if you don't feel safe or if you think someone else might not be safe.

- Check that children have a good concept of rules/ laws and the need for someone to make sure that people follow them. Explain that this is a role for the police.

- Talk about children's prior knowledge and experience of the police, emphasising their role in keeping people safe.

While you share the book:

- Help children to read some of the more unfamiliar words.

- Talk about the questions. Encourage children to make links between their own experiences and the information in the book.

- Talk about the police in your locality. Where are they? What are they doing?

After you have shared the book:

- If possible, take children to visit a police station, or invite a police officer to come and talk to the class.

- Make a list of all the different jobs that police officers do.

- Talk about reasons why people might become police officers.

- Work through the free activity sheets at www.hachetteschools.co.uk

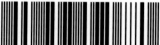
Citizenship through informed and responsible action

Ruth Ibegbuna & Laura Pottinger
Series Editor: Peter Brett

Acknowledgements

p. 16 The Ten Commandments, Exodus 20, The New English Bible (Oxford University Press, 1994); p. 17 Black Panther Party: The Ten Point Program © The Dr. Huey P. Newton Foundation Inc.; p. 29 Life expectancy in Angola from Central Intelligence Agency (CIA) World Factbook www.cia.gov/library/publications/the-world-factbook; p. 38 (top) © Dinodia Images/Alamy, (bottom) © iStockphoto.com/konstantin32; p. 39 (top) © Kathy deWitt/Alamy, (bottom) © Roger Hutchings/Alamy; p. 54 Reproduced by kind permission of the Earl Spencer © The Ninth Earl Spencer; p. 63 (bottom) 'Miracle on the Hudson: 155 survive crash as jet hits river in New York', Ed Pilkington, 16 January 2009. Copyright Guardian News & Media Ltd 2009; p. 64 (text top) 'We are a nation reborn', Andrew Rawnsley, 03 May 1997. Copyright Guardian News & Media Ltd 1997, (photo top) © Trinity Mirror/Mirrorpix/Alamy, (text bottom) 'The New Prime Minister: Gordon Brown', Nicholas Watt, 01 July 2007. Copyright Guardian News & Media Ltd 2007, (photo bottom) © Murray Sanders/Murray Sanders/Rex Features; p. 68 © Richard Young/Rex Features; p. 70 (top) © Rex Features, (bottom) © Darren Fletcher/Rex Features

© 2009 Folens Limited, on behalf of the authors.

United Kingdom: Folens Publishers, Waterslade House, Thame Road, Haddenham, Buckinghamshire, HP17 8NT.
Email: folens@folens.com Website: www.folens.com

Ireland: Folens Publishers, Greenhills Road, Tallaght, Dublin 24.
Email: info@folens.ie Website: www.folens.ie

Layout artist: Planman Technologies
Cover design: Jump To
Illustrations: Janet Baker (JB Illustrations)

The websites recommended in this publication were correct at the time of going to press, however websites may have been removed or web addresses changed since that time. Folens has made every attempt to suggest websites that are reliable and appropriate for student's use. It is not unknown for unscrupulous individuals to put unsuitable material on websites that may be accessed by students. Teachers should check all websites before allowing students to access them. Folens is not responsible for the content of external websites.

For general spellings Folens adheres to Oxford Dictionary of English, Second Edition (Revised), 2005.

First published 2009 by Folens Limited.

Every effort has been made to contact copyright holders of material used in this publication. If any copyright holder has been overlooked, we will be pleased to make any necessary arrangements.

British Library Cataloguing in Publication Data. A catalogue record for this publication is available from the British Library.

ISBN 978-1-85008-447-1   Folens code FD4471